BA

Alan Du̲ra̲... ̲ was
eight. O̲... ̲g for
two seasons in the Collingwood Boys Junior
School football team, scoring one goal! After
that, it was all downhill. He supports Manchester
United and his favourite player of all time is
George Best, after whom he named his one and
only goldfish. Sadly, the goldfish died. He has
passed his football talents on to his son Kit, who
plays in a little league – and around the house
with a pair of rolled-up socks. Bad Boyz is based
on children Alan has met during his career as an
author and football spectator ... you know who
you are!

Alan Durant's football stories have appeared in
various anthologies, including two collections of
Gary Lineker's Favourite Football Stories; *On Me
'Ead, Santa*; and *Football Shorts*. He is also the
author of the Leggs United series about a family
football team managed by a ghost. The series and
Alan himself were featured in a recent Children's
Bafta Award-winning programme on BBC TV. His
other work ranges from picture books for young
children to novels and mystery stories for young
adults. Alan lives just south of London with his
wife, Jinny, and three children, Amy, Kit and
Josie. He doesn't expect to get a call from Sven
Goran Eriksson.

Books by the same author

Bad Boyz: Kicking Off
Leagues Apart
K.O. Kings
Creepe Hall
Return to Creepe Hall
Creepe Hall For Ever!
Jake's Magic
Star Quest: Voyage to the Greylon Galaxy
Spider McDrew
Happy Birthday, Spider McDrew
Little Troll
Little Troll and the Big Present
Leggs United (series)
Football Fun

BAD BOYZ: BARMY ARMY

ALAN DURANT

WALKER BOOKS
AND SUBSIDIARIES

LONDON · BOSTON · SYDNEY · AUCKLAND

First published 2002 by Walker Books Ltd
87 Vauxhall Walk, London SE11 5HJ

4 6 8 10 9 7 5

Text © 2002 Alan Durant
Bad Boyz logo © 2001 Phil Schramm
Cover photography by Cliff Birtchell
Cover design by Walker Books Ltd

This book has been typeset in Futura book

Printed and bound in Great Britain by
J. H. Haynes & Co. Ltd. Sparkford

British Library Cataloguing in Publication Data:
a catalogue record for this book is
available from the British Library

ISBN 0-7445-5992-8

*For my footballing nephew Max Lyon and –
across the Channel – pour la famille Poupart
avec mes sentiments les plus amicaux.
Vive le football!*

1

"Bonjour, mes choux! J'ai des bonnes nouvelles. Nous allons jouer au football en France!"

Mr Davies beamed out at the seven children sitting in front of him in the classroom. Together, they made up the little league football team Bad Boyz. As well as being the children's teacher at school, Mr Davies was the Bad Boyz manager. At this moment, his team were all gaping back at him as if he'd just grown purple fins.

"Eh?" grunted Kyle, the Bad Boyz keeper, at last.

"Are you all right, sir?" enquired Dareth, the team's skipper. "Would yer like some water or sumfing?"

Mr Davies shook his head. "I was speaking French," he explained.

"Oh yeah, *bonjour,*" Jordan nodded. "I

know that. I saw it tagged on a wall in town somewhere." Jordan was very keen on graffiti. Her tagging exploits had got her into a lot of trouble in the past.

"It means 'good day'," said Mr Davies: "hello."

"'Ello," Dareth responded with a broad grin.

Mr Davies ignored him. "I was telling you that I had some good news," he went on. "We're going to play football in France."

"In France?" squeaked Bloomer, his cheeks flaring pink. "That's ... well ... it's ... not in this country, is it?"

"Duh, well done, Bloomer!" Jordan scoffed. "Of course it's not in this country. It's a completely *different* country."

"We're going to France, we're going to France!" exclaimed Max dramatically, and he banged his head down on the desk in a pretend faint.

Sung-Woo put up his hand.

"Yes, Sung-Woo?" said Mr Davies.

Sung-Woo frowned. "I no understand," he muttered seriously, "why you say hello to your shoe."

8

"Yeah, you did, sir," piped Bloomer. "You said 'bonjewer my shoe'."

"*Bonjour*, mes choux," Mr Davies corrected him. "It's a term of endearment the French use. It means 'Hello, my cabbages'."

"Eh? You what?" Kyle uttered. "We ain't cabbages."

"No," agreed Bloomer shrilly, "we're not vegetables."

"*We* aren't," said Jordan, "*you* are."

"No, we all are," said Max surprisingly.

"What d'yer mean?" Kyle demanded. His podgy face crinkled like a deflating beach ball.

"Well, we're human *beans*. Get it?" Max declared. He rolled his eyes and stuck out his tongue.

Everyone laughed except Sung-Woo, who looked more confused than ever.

"It was a joke, Sung-Woo," said Mr Davies. He raised his eyebrows at Max. "And not a very good one. Now let's get back to the subject... The Appleton Little League has a link with a similar league in France. They've invited us, as little league champions, to go to France to play two matches against the

9

winners of their league. A sort of continental championship, I suppose. What do you say to that?" His gaze fell on Sadiq. "Sadiq, you've been very quiet," he said. "What do you think?"

Sadiq was rarely slow in voicing his opinion to teachers – or anyone else, come to that. It had often got him into detention. Today, though, he had been unusually silent.

"Yeah, it sounds all right," he said without enthusiasm.

"All right?" queried Mr Davies. "Is that the best you can do?"

Sadiq shrugged. "It sounds good," he ventured, but still without real enthusiasm.

"It sounds wicked," Dareth asserted. "I've never been to France."

"Have any of you ever been abroad?" Mr Davies asked. "Apart from Sung-Woo." Sung-Woo had lived abroad until less than a year ago.

"I been to Spain," said Jordan.

"Me too," squawked Bloomer.

"I been to Greece," said Max. "Grease Lightning," he sang, and started to jig around in a weird kind of dance.

Mr Davies raised his eyes again. "Anyone else?" he prompted.

Dareth put up his hand. "I've been to Iceland," he said. He ran his hand over his cropped head and grinned. "Me gran gets her frozen sausages there."

Mr Davies shook his head and sighed.

2

There was a lot to be done to prepare for the trip to France. Mr Davies wrote a letter to all the parents giving them details and inviting them to a meeting at the Appleton Little League headquarters. This was, in fact, a wooden scout hut. On the evening of the meeting there was just about enough room to squeeze everyone in.

There was at least one parent of each child present – with the exception of Dareth's and Bloomer's. Dareth's mum was still off on her long "holiday", so his gran came instead – Mr Davies half expected her to bring her beloved budgie Rameses with her, but she didn't. Bloomer's mum and stepdad were both at work, so Bloomer came with his uncle.

Mr Davies began the meeting by welcoming

everyone and giving a brief introduction: how the trip to France had come about, when they'd be setting off, where exactly they were going… Then he asked if there were any questions.

Dareth's gran was the first to speak. "I'm not sure about this going to France," she said. She looked around at the rest of the gathering with a narrow-eyed frown. "Well, they eat frogs there, don't they?" she went on. There was some laughter.

"Only the legs," said Mr Davies with a smile. "But don't worry, Mrs Nesbitt. We won't be eating any frogs, I can assure you. It's not really footballers' food."

"It's not any sort of food, if yer ask me," tutted Dareth's gran. "You wouldn't get me touching it, that's for sure. Frogs!" Her frown deepened into a look of fierce disgust.

"You like toad-in-the-hole, Gran," Dareth remarked with a smirk.

Max and Bloomer laughed.

"Don't be cheeky," said Dareth's gran. But she didn't say any more.

Max's dad wanted to know about the cost of the trip. "How much are we going to have to pay?" he asked.

Mr Davies had expected this question. "Very little," he was pleased to report. Then he went on to explain that the Appleton Little League was paying for the team's travel out of its funds, while the accommodation and food were being provided free of charge by the French Little League. The children's school had done its bit, too, by lending its minibus. "So all you'll need to pay out is some spending money for the children."

This was met by a general murmur of approval.

"That sounds very reasonable," said Max's dad. He turned to his son. "You'd better get yourself up on Saturday mornings and help me with my round," he said, "if you want to earn some money." Max's dad was a milkman. The company he worked for, the Doorstep Dairy, was Bad Boyz' kit sponsor.

"I help you already," declared Max with unusual seriousness.

"No, you sometimes come with me and pretend to shoot people with the milk bottles," said Max's dad. "That's not the same thing as helping."

Max hung his head and pulled a long face

in mock shame.

The next to speak was Jordan's dad. He was a little worried, he said, about Jordan being the only girl on the trip.

"Dad!" Jordan snapped. She was one of the strongest characters in the team and more than capable of looking after herself.

"It's all right, Jordan," said Mr Davies. "I think your dad's made a fair point. I know you can do everything the boys can do – and more. But you aren't a boy."

"Nah, she's a cabbage," said Kyle with a fleshy grin.

Jordan gave him a withering glare.

"She's a girl," said Mr Davies. "We're a mixed-sex team. Which is why I've asked a friend of mine to come and help me look after you." He looked across at a young woman sitting at the back of the hut. Like him, she was dressed in jogging trousers and a hooded sweatshirt. "Would you like to come up and join me, Miss Rogers?" he said. There was a buzz of excitement among the assembled Bad Boyz as the woman got up and walked to the front of the room.

"This is Julie Rogers," said Mr Davies.

"She's also a teacher, in another school, and she's agreed to come with us to make sure we don't get into any trouble. Isn't that right, Julie?"

"I'll do my best," she said pleasantly.

This was enough for Jordan's dad: his worries were put to rest. He was happy for Jordan to go, he said.

Bloomer's uncle had a question. He wondered how long the team was going to be away.

"Four days," Mr Davies informed him.

Bloomer's uncle frowned as if there was a problem.

"Is there something wrong?" Mr Davies asked.

"Oh no," said Bloomer's uncle with a casual wag of his head. "I was just hoping it might be a bit longer, that's all." Everyone laughed. Bloomer's cheeks went a brighter shade of scarlet.

"I'm sure his mum wouldn't want him to be away any longer," said Miss Rogers sweetly, which made Bloomer's cheeks blush even more. But it brought a smile to his face too.

Sadiq's mum didn't say anything during the

meeting, but at the end, when all the others had gone, she came up to Mr Davies.

"Hi," Mr Davies greeted her. "We haven't met before, have we?"

Sadiq's mum shook her head. She looked agitated. "I don't want my son to go," she stated simply.

"Oh," said Mr Davies. He was completely taken aback. "Why?"

"I need him at home," said Sadiq's mum.

"It's only for four days, Mrs Ali," Mr Davies pointed out. "And it'll be a great experience for Sadiq."

"I need him here," she insisted. "And anyway, what if they didn't let him back into the country? It happens, you know. These customs people are very racist. They turn black people away all the time."

"That's immigration, Mrs Ali," Mr Davies reasoned. "Sadiq *lives* here. No one's going to stop him coming back to his home."

"I don't know," said Sadiq's mum. "I worry about Sadiq. He's my only boy. He gets very homesick, you know. He needs his mother to look after him." She looked anxiously at Sadiq, who was standing, head down, at her side.

17

He was clearly not enjoying the conversation.

It was Miss Rogers who came to his rescue. "We'll look after Sadiq, Mrs Ali," she said. "I know it's not the same as having his mum around, but I promise I'll look out for him. I'll see he's all right." She smiled a very reassuring smile – and Mr Davies gave himself a mental pat on the back for inviting her.

Sadiq's mum wasn't entirely convinced, but she was won over enough eventually to agree to let Sadiq join the trip. At least that meant Bad Boyz would go to France with a complete team – presuming there were no disasters between now and their departure.

But then, of course, with Bad Boyz that was a big presumption to make...

3

Preparations for the trip were in full swing. Mr Davies made sure everyone had either a passport or a form to get hold of one. In a couple of cases, where he knew reading the forms would be a problem, he helped to fill them in.

The team had a smart playing strip, but Mr Davies thought they should have a team item to wear off the field while they were away. Max suggested a Bad Boyz on tour T-shirt. Jordan could design it, he said – and everyone agreed. The next day, Jordan brought in her design. The Bad Boyz lettering was written in spray-paint with a football replacing the "o" in "Boyz". Not surprisingly, it looked like graffiti. Her team-mates were well impressed.

"That looks really professional," Kyle remarked.

"Yeah, we're gonna look real cool," said Dareth.

"Like, er, cucumbers," said Bloomer.

Jordan smiled. "Well, it's better than being cabbages, I suppose," she said.

Mr Davies said he knew someone who would print the T-shirts for them. He even got Piranha, the head-teacher, to pay for them.

Everything was going fine … until the day before the trip, when Dareth informed Mr Davies that he didn't have a passport.

"But I sorted out all the forms for you," Mr Davies said. "Didn't you send them off to the Passport Office?"

"Course I did!" Dareth exclaimed, as if he was Mr Reliable. Mr Davies knew he was actually about as reliable as a torch without batteries. "They just 'aven't come back."

Mr Davies made some frantic enquiries over the phone. The passport had been sent over a week ago, he was assured. There weren't any problems with the post in the area, so it should certainly have arrived by now. But the fact was, it hadn't. Suddenly Mr Davies had an idea why not.

He found Dareth at lunchtime. "Dareth,

when you filled in the passport form, did you put down your address?"

Once again, Dareth looked aggrieved. "Course I did," he said. "I ain't stupid."

"I know you're not, Dareth," said Mr Davies. "But what address did you put?"

"Mine, of course," said Dareth. "What d'you think I put down – Buckingham Palace?"

Mr Davies smiled. "You put down your mum's address, right?" he pressed.

"Yeah," said Dareth. "That's me 'ome, innit?"

"But you don't live there, do you." Mr Davies pointed out. "Not at the moment. You live with your gran."

A sheepish grin appeared on Dareth's face. "Me passport's at 'ome," he said. "I never thought of that."

After school, Mr Davies gave Dareth a lift to his mum's flat – and there, among the small mound of junk mail, bills and letters was a brown envelope containing Dareth's passport. The crisis was over.

But there was another to come.

The day of the trip, one by one the Bad Boyz players arrived, proudly wearing their new

21

T-shirts. They gave their bags to Mr Davies, who packed them in the minibus. Miss Rogers, meanwhile, collected up the passports. The team was supposed to set off at nine o'clock. But at twenty past, Sadiq had still not arrived. Everyone else was in the minibus, ready to go.

"We'll pick him up on the way," Mr Davies decided. He had a sinking feeling as he drove. He couldn't help recalling his conversation with Sadiq's mum. What if she'd changed her mind again at the last minute and wouldn't let Sadiq come? But that, as they discovered on arriving at Sadiq's house, wasn't the problem. The problem was Sadiq himself. He didn't want to go.

"But why, Sadiq?" Mr Davies asked – pleaded, almost.

Sadiq shrugged. "I just don't want to," he said.

"But the others are relying on you. You can't pull out now."

"I don't want to go," Sadiq insisted. He looked really miserable.

"Can I have a word with Sadiq?" Miss Rogers asked. "Just the two of us?"

Mr Davies looked surprised. "Yeah, sure," he said. "I'd better go and check on the others anyway," he added. He smiled. "If they haven't driven off and left us..." He went outside to the minibus.

Ten minutes later there was a huge cheer in the minibus as Miss Rogers and Sadiq appeared. Sadiq didn't exactly look ecstatic. But he didn't look miserable, either. Once again Mr Davies congratulated himself on inviting his friend along.

While Sadiq took his seat, Mr Davies helped Miss Rogers with the luggage.

"How did you sort that?" he asked with admiration.

"He's nervous," she explained. "He's never been away from home before. I think he's scared he'll make a fool of himself. I said I'd see that he didn't."

"And that swung it?" said Mr Davies admiringly.

"Well, not just that."

"What else, then?" Mr Davies was genuinely intrigued.

Miss Rogers grinned. "I told him you used to be just the same," she said.

4

The trip to the ferry was a happy one. There was a lot of singing and shouting and general high-spiritedness. Even Sung-Woo joined in. He didn't actually laugh – he never did – but once or twice he smiled broadly. He had a surprise for them all too. He'd brought some cakes, he said, for the journey.

"Get 'em out then," Kyle urged. "I never had no breakfast this morning."

"Yeah, let's have a cake," piped Bloomer.

Sung-Woo rummaged around in the small rucksack at his feet and pulled out something in a polystyrene tray covered in clingfilm.

His team-mates stared at the tray with bewilderment. Its contents looked a bit like a collection of pebbly, rocky things you might find at the beach. Some of them were green, some sandy-brown, some white. There were also a couple of thick, white slabs and some creamy pasta-like things shaped like bowler hats.

"What's that?" asked Dareth at last.

"Cakes," said Sung-Woo happily.

"That ain't cakes," Kyle grumbled. His face glooped into a scowl of disappointment.

"Yes," insisted Sung-Woo. "They is cakes. Is made with rice." He tore away the cellophane wrapping and offered them to the others.

Max was the first to try one. He picked up a piece of something sprinkled with what looked like chocolate. He took a bite and, after appearing to enjoy it for a second or two, contorted his face into a cross-eyed grimace. His hand went to his throat.

"I think I've ... been ... poisoned," he gasped, and his head sagged as if he were dead. Dareth and Bloomer laughed.

"I'll try a bit," said Jordan. She tasted another cake that had a bean in it. She swallowed hard. "Umm, very ... interesting," she said. "Thanks, Sung-Woo."

"You want some more?" Sung-Woo asked hopefully.

"No thanks," said Jordan.

25

"I'll 'ave some," said Kyle. He took one of the green cakes. "This is all right," he said. "It's a bit like cold rice pudding. Only it's green."

"I had green pudding once," said Bloomer. "It was apple pudding."

"Well, duh, apples are green," said Jordan. But Bloomer wasn't listening. He'd spotted something through the window. "Look, there's a cow!" he shrieked, and he started to moo. He was soon joined by Dareth and Max. Kyle, meanwhile, munched his way through the tray of rice cakes. Long before they reached the ferry he'd eaten the lot.

Later, he wished he hadn't. Half an hour into the ferry crossing, he was violently sick. Luckily he was leaning over the side of the boat at the time.

"I think the seagulls like your rice cakes, Sung-Woo," Dareth remarked with a nod at the swooping gulls.

"Ugh, that's sick," said Jordan.

"Yeah, it is," Dareth agreed.

Fortunately, it wasn't a rough crossing and no one else felt ill. At times Mr Davies almost wished they had – it might have calmed them down a bit. He spent most of the time trying to stop them from throwing themselves, one another or any of their possessions overboard, or upsetting the other passengers with their rowdy behaviour – when they weren't sneaking off to the toddlers' play area or *Le Pub*. When the call came for them to rejoin their vehicles, the Bad Boyz coach breathed a sigh of relief – until he realized he'd lost Bloomer.

While Miss Rogers took the others down to the minibus, Mr Davies searched for his missing player. Eventually he found Bloomer by a slot-machine.

"Bloomer, what are you doing? You should be on the bus!" Bloomer started punching the buttons on the machine like a maniac. He clearly hadn't put any money in, though, because nothing happened. "You're not allowed to play on this machine, Bloomer," Mr Davies remarked sternly, nodding at the sign over the machine. It read GAMING MACHINE: PLAYERS MUST BE OVER 18 YEARS OF AGE. "You're not old enough."

"I'm not playing," Bloomer argued. "I'm … practising."

"Practising for what?"

"For when I'm older," said Bloomer.

Mr Davies sighed with exasperation. "Bloomer," he said, "if you don't get down those stairs right now, you won't be getting any older."

5

There was a great cheer when the minibus drove off the ferry at Calais. Even Sadiq joined in. After a quiet start to the journey, he seemed happy enough. He hadn't shown any signs of homesickness so far, which was a relief to Mr Davies.

It was only an hour's drive from the ferry to the farm on which the team were to stay. As they approached, Mr Davies pointed out the sign for the local town, Menuer.

"That's where the little league is," he said.

Max pinched his nose with his thumb and finger as if he smelt something bad.

"Why you doing that?" Dareth asked. "You haven't farted again, Kyle, have you?"

"What? I never did nuffing," Kyle grumbled.

"No, didn't you read the sign?" Max said.

29

"It said manure." He screwed up his face in an expression of massive disgust. "We're going to be playing in manure."

The others laughed.

"It's not manure, Max," Mr Davies corrected him. "It's Men-u-eh."

"Don't they teach you anything at school?" Miss Rogers added teasingly.

Minutes later, they drove into the farmyard. As they drew up in front of the large farmhouse, their hosts – the farmer, his wife and three children – came out to meet them.

The Bad Boyz party got out of the minibus and introductions were made. The farmer and his wife were called Monsieur and Madame Champs. They spoke very good English.

"We are the champs," joked Monsieur Champs.

Mr Davies explained to his team that although the farmer's name was spelt "champs", it was pronounced more like *"shom"*. "In English *champs* means fields," he said.

The farmer nodded. "And these are our children," he said. "The little fields: Louis, Laura and Vincent."

"Louis and Laura are in the football team," added Madame Champs. "Vincent is a bit young."

"He 'elps the manager," said Monsieur Champs. He smiled broadly. "That's me."

Mr Davies introduced himself and Miss Rogers and each member of his team in turn. Everyone shook hands.

"We 'ope you will be very 'appy 'ere," said Monsieur Champs warmly.

Mr Davies and Miss Rogers had rooms in the farmhouse, but the Bad Boyz were to sleep in a large barn that was attached to it. Monsieur Champs took them to see it. It had been done up like a dormitory with seven beds – four along one wall and three along the opposite wall.

The farmer glanced at Jordan a little sheepishly. "I did not know you 'ad a girl in your team too," he said. "Perhaps she would like to sleep in the 'ouse. She could share Laura's room…"

Jordan shook her head vehemently. "No, I want to sleep here," she said. She threw her bag onto one of the beds. "That's mine," she declared.

"Ah, you are one of the boys," smiled the farmer. "I 'ope you are not bad like them."

Monsieur Champs may only have been making a joke on the team's name, but they took it as a compliment, grinning hugely.

Dareth nodded at Jordan. "She's really bad," he said. "She's nearly as bad as me."

"And me," squeaked Bloomer. "I'm very bad."

Jordan shook her head with a wry smile. "Nah, you're not bad, Bloomer," she said. "You're pants."

The rest of the team laughed, while the farmer looked on bemused – until Mr Davies explained that Jordan wasn't calling Bloomer underwear; pants meant "no good – rubbish."

"Ah, I see," said the farmer. He smiled. "Like Manchester City."

6

After they'd settled in, and Mr Davies and Miss Rogers were having a cup of tea with Monsieur and Madame Champs, Bad Boyz were given a tour of the farm by the farmer's children. Their English wasn't as good as their parents', but it was a lot better than their guests' French!

There were some chickens on the farm – to provide the family with fresh eggs – but these were the only animals, apart from Vincent's pet rabbit.

"We grow *légumes*," said Louis, pointing out at the fields around the farm. "Vegetables."

"Do you grow shoes?" asked Max.

Louis looked down at his feet. "Shoes?" he queried.

33

"Shoe," Jordan chipped in. "You know, cabbage."

"Ah, cabbage," Louis smiled. Then he shook his head. "No," he said.

His sister took over: "We grow beetroot and potatoes and parrots," she said.

As one, Bad Boyz fell into a fit of the giggles.

Laura blushed. "I mean carrots," she corrected herself. "My English very bad."

"No, it ain't," said Kyle encouragingly. "It's wicked." Once again, the three French children looked totally confused.

"He means your English is very good," Dareth explained.

"Ah, thank you," Laura said, and blushed even more.

The English children were very impressed by the farm with all its outhouses and fields. It was a huge contrast to the concrete urban estates on which most of the Bad Boyz lived. They especially liked all the heavy farming machinery; there were several tractors with a variety of attachments and a massive combine harvester. Louis invited his guests to have a go at sitting up in the driver's seat. When Max took his turn at the wheel he made very noisy sound effects as if he was actually driving the vehicle. Only it sounded more like he was driving a Formula One racing car than a combine harvester.

"This is well cool," he enthused.

"Well, it's a bit more exciting than a milk float," said Sadiq.

"Max's dad's a milkman," explained Jordan.

Another interesting discovery was a large pond behind the barn in which Bad Boyz were staying. It wasn't very deep, but you could swim in it, Louis said. There was a small boat, too, with a single sculling oar.

"That's Vincent's," said Louis, "but you can use it if you want."

"Cheers," said Dareth. He grinned at Vincent, but the small French boy didn't respond. In fact, he showed no real sign of emotion at all until they reached the large "cage" where the pet rabbit was kept. Then his whole manner changed. In a moment he was inside the cage; and in another he was holding the rabbit in his arms and feeding it some leaves. The large, furry rabbit nibbled happily.

"*Tu as faim, Caramel,*" Vincent cooed. "*Manges, mon petit, manges.*"

"Vincent doesn't talk much," said Laura. "Only to Caramel, his rabbit."

"Sung-Woo don't talk much neither," said Kyle. "Only he ain't got a rabbit."

Sung-Woo half smiled, but he didn't say anything.

"I wish I had a rabbit," piped Bloomer. "I love rabbits." His hamster had died a few months before and now he hadn't got a pet. He'd found a rat out by his dustbin, but he hadn't been able to keep it.

"You can't keep a rabbit in a block of flats," Sadiq pointed out. "Where would you put it?"

Two rosy circles appeared on Bloomer's cheeks. "I'd keep it in me hamster cage," he declared hotly. "It could play on the wheel."

"Bloomer, you dir," Jordan scoffed. "Rabbits don't play on wheels. And anyway, look at the size of that rabbit." She nodded at Caramel, cradled in Vincent's arms. "He's much too big to fit in a hamster cage."

"Yeah, well," Bloomer muttered sulkily. But he soon perked up when Vincent asked him if he'd like to hold Caramel. In a shot, he joined the French boy in the cage. While the others looked on, Vincent showed Bloomer how to hold the rabbit and passed him some leaves so that he could feed it. Bloomer was a picture of contentment.

"These are dandelion leaves, aren't they?" he squeaked.

"In France, we call them *pis-en-lit*," said Louis with a big smile. "You know, pee in the bed."

Bad Boyz took in this bit of French with great delight. In fact, they repeated it as often as possible throughout the rest of the day. It was amazing, Mr Davies remarked to Miss Rogers when they'd settled the children in bed that evening, that they struggled to say hello in French but could all say dandelion perfectly.

"As long as they only say it," Miss Rogers remarked, looking down the row of tucked-up children. "And don't do it."

"If wet beds are the worst trouble we have on this trip, I'll be quite happy," Mr Davies replied. Then he wished his team goodnight.

7

As it happened, the next time Mr Davies saw his team they *were* all completely wet – not in their beds but in the pond. The sound of their splashing and shrieking brought him out of the house – and there they all were, having a whale of a time. Sung-Woo and Jordan were in the boat and the others were trying to capsize them. As Mr Davies looked on, the farmer's children dashed past him and plunged into the pond to join in the fun. Mr Davies retreated to the house for a cup of coffee.

The sun shone through the morning and all looked set fair for the afternoon's match between the two little league champions. Then just after lunch the skies closed in, turning from a mottled blue to a heavy grey, and it started to pour. For an hour or so, the rain hammered down as if it was trying to bring back Noah's flood. Mr Davies feared that the match would have to be cancelled, but Monsieur Champs was quite relaxed. "It's just a shower," he said. "It will clear soon." He was right.

When the rain stopped, the farmer and Mr Davies went out to test the ground. It was a little soft, but not too bad. There had not been much rain recently and so the ground was quite firm. They were confident the pitch would be in a good enough condition to play on.

At half past two, the Bad Boyz clambered into the minibus dressed in their strip and set off for the ground, following Monsieur Champs and family. They drove along a narrow road through fields. They only saw one other vehicle and that was a moped, ridden by a teenage boy. As they passed, the boy made a rude gesture; in response, Max dropped his shorts and did a moony. The moped wobbled for an instant and nearly went off into a ditch, but luckily its rider just managed to keep control. The Bad Boyz players whooped with laughter.

"What's going on back there?" Mr Davies enquired.

"Oh, nothing," said Dareth casually. "Max just did something funny."

"Tell me something new," said Mr Davies.

At last they reached the Menuer Little League ground. It was a park on the outskirts of the town. A sign outside said *"Bienvenue Les Bad Boyz!"*, and over each of the park gates were draped an English and a French flag.

"Sir!" squawked Bloomer urgently. "They've got a Union Jack!"

"Yes, I know," said Mr Davies. "It's to welcome us. That's what that sign says, 'Welcome, Bad Boyz'."

"That's nice," said Miss Rogers. "Everyone is so friendly." Just as she said this, the moped rider sped by. He tooted his horn and swore in English. Fortunately his accent was terrible and neither Mr Davies or Miss Rogers understood him.

"I think he's welcoming us to France," Dareth said cheerily, knowing that exactly the opposite was true.

Apart from Louis and Laura, the other members of the French team, Les Bleus, were waiting when the farmer drew up in the carpark. In keeping with their name, Les Bleus were dressed in smart royal-blue tracksuits.

When everyone had got out of their vehicles, Monsieur Champs introduced the rest of his team to the guests. He nodded at the pitch before them. "It looks as if we have many people today, despite the rain."

It was true: the pitch was completely surrounded by spectators. Bad Boyz were quite taken aback. On a normal Saturday at home their games didn't even attract enough of a crowd to cover one end of the pitch, never mind all four sides.

"Do you get crowds like this every week?" Mr Davies asked.

The farmer laughed. "No," he said. "But when it's a match against the English..." He shrugged expressively.

"Well, let's hope we can put on a good show for them," Mr Davies remarked. Even he was feeling a little overwhelmed at the size of the crowd.

The two teams went through their warming-up routines of stretching and jogging, passing and shooting. It was as they were doing this last exercise that Mr Davies noticed that while all the others had changed into boots, Kyle was still wearing trainers.

"Kyle, why aren't you wearing your boots?" he said. "You'll need them on this slippery grass."

Kyle looked at his manager with a face of gloom. "I ain't got no boots," he said unhappily. "Me last pair ripped and me mum said she couldn't afford to buy me no more."

Mr Davies sighed. "I wish you'd said before we left. I could have sorted something out for you." He felt the grass with one foot. "At least it's not too muddy," he said, adding more in hope than belief, "You'll be all right."

8

It was a tight game from the start. The two teams were well-matched and both seemed a little nervous, as if in awe of the occasion and the crowd. All but two of the spectators – Mr Davies and Miss Rogers – were supporting the home team, but they were also quick to applaud and cheer any good piece of play by the visitors. Stan Reynolds, the Appleton Little League secretary, would have been proud of them. Good sportsmanship by players and spectators alike was high up on the list of the league's priorities. Mr Reynolds would also have been delighted with Bad Boyz, whose behaviour was much better than their name implied. In fact, there was hardly a foul in the entire first half. There were some good passing moves and some nice flashes of skill, but

43

neither side looked very dangerous. At half-time the score was 0–0. There had been few chances and Kyle had barely had to make a save. Cerainly he hadn't been tested – nor had his opposite number on the French side. Sung-Woo and Dareth, in particular, were having very quiet games.

"We need to crank this up a bit," said Mr Davies during the interval, while Miss Rogers passed round segments of orange that Madame Champs had given her. "I know it's a friendly competition, but we still want to win, don't we?" The players nodded, without being entirely convincing. "Let's get some more pace into our game," the coach continued. "You've given them respect … now destroy them!" He deliberately went over the top to grab their attention. And it worked – except with Bloomer. He was gazing in the opposite direction. "Bloomer! We're over here. What are you looking at?"

Bloomer turned, his cheeks flushing pink. "I thought I saw a rabbit," he said.

Mr Davies shook his head and sighed. "Could you just try and forget about rabbits, Bloomer, for the next twenty-five minutes, and concentrate on football?"

"Yes, sir," Bloomer squeaked. But for Bloomer twenty-five minutes was a very long time indeed – given that his normal attention span was about thirty seconds. His team-mates were used to having to shout at him at frequent intervals, but today he was even worse than usual and they were less in the mood for shouting. Which meant he made a lot of mistakes. During the first half he'd often been standing in the wrong place or facing the wrong way and he'd given the ball away on several occasions. This continued in the second half.

Bloomer's inattention wasn't the only handicap that Bad Boyz had to cope with, either. Their progress was also hampered by a sudden and severe change in the weather. The second half had barely kicked off when the rain started to hammer down once more. While conditions were the same for both sides, the slope of the pitch encouraged the water to settle around the end that Bad Boyz were defending. Keeping balanced became difficult enough for players with boots on, but for Kyle, wearing worn trainers, it was soon a serious problem. It was only a matter of time before disaster struck.

For ten minutes, Bad Boyz held out, despite slipping and sliding – Sung-Woo even managed to get a powerful shot on target. Unfortunately for him it went straight at the French keeper, who did well to hold onto the ball. He quickly launched it upfield. Jordan jumped to head the ball clear, but mistimed her leap and it bounced off her head, back towards her own team's goal. The ball fell midway between Louis and Sadiq, and both sprinted after it. The French boy got to the ball first, and kicking the ball on, bore down on the Bad Boyz goal. For a moment it looked as if he'd be clean through with only Kyle to beat. But to his credit, Sadiq got back and made a sliding challenge to push the ball towards his advancing keeper.

Kyle reacted quickly, rushing forward to get to the ball before Louis could reach it. But, as he kicked at the ball to boot it clear, his standing foot slipped from under him and he fell flat on his back in the mud. The ball, meanwhile, continued on its journey towards the Bad Boyz goal – as did Louis. By the time he caught up with the ball, though, it had already rolled over the goal line. Louis crashed it into the net anyway with great glee, before turning with his arms raised to start the goal celebrations.

Sadiq was furious. "Kyle, you fat lump, what're you doing?" he hissed, as he got to his feet. "You should have cleared that easy."

Kyle sat up in the mud with an angry scowl. "Just shut up!" he growled. "It weren't my fault. I slipped, didn't I? You shoulda cleared it."

"I got my tackle in," Sadiq persisted, moving towards Kyle. "All you had to do was kick the ball away."

"Well, I couldn't, could I! I was on me back."

"On your great fat arse, more like," Sadiq muttered.

The two boys were face to face now and on the verge of coming to blows. It was like a return to the bad old days when they fought regularly.

"Break it up, you two!" Mr Davies shouted from the touch-line, but he was too far away to stop the trouble. Luckily Jordan and Dareth stepped in and separated their warring team-mates.

But the damage was done. The next fifteen minutes were a nightmare for Bad Boyz. Even the rain stopping failed to inspire them. They were in total disarray and the home team took full advantage, knocking in three more goals before the end of the game. The final score was 4–0 to Les Bleus. Bad Boyz had been routed.

9

During the drive back to the farm in the minibus, hardly a word was spoken. Muddy and wet and bedraggled, Bad Boyz looked as if they'd happily go back to England right there and then. Fortunately, their hosts were very kind and generous in victory. There was no gloating. Indeed, they seemed almost as upset as their guests at the way the match had gone.

"Tomorrow is another day," said Monsieur Champs when they arrived back at the farm. "Maybe it will not go so well for us. *On verra.* We shall see." He smiled at Bad Boyz. "But now, what you all need is a nice hot shower, no?"

That is exactly what Bad Boyz needed, and afterwards, sitting down to a huge tea in the farmhouse kitchen, warm and clean, they looked much more themselves. All except Sadiq. He continued to look as miserable as could be. He even managed to make eating a sumptuous chocolate eclair appear like a form of torture, and made Sung-Woo look jolly.

Mr Davies watched Sadiq nervously. Once again he was glad he had Julie Rogers with him. He had a feeling she was going to have a very important role to play that evening.

After tea, Bad Boyz were taken to Crecy, the site of a famous battle between France and England. They climbed a wooden tower, which had been built on the spot where a windmill had once stood, and from where King Edward the Third had surveyed the fighting.

"The French suffered a terrible defeat," said Monsieur Champs. He went on to explain that although the French had greater numbers and expected to win, the English had a devastating new weapon: the longbow. The English archers destroyed the French army with their arrows.

Usually, a trip to a battlefield would have been Bad Boyz' idea of a perfect outing. They'd have liked nothing better than the opportunity to re-enact, very noisily, a famous battle –

especially one that the English had won. But it was a measure of how subdued they were that evening that they simply looked and listened. Well, all except Max, who was incapable of simply looking and listening. He stood at the top of the tower and pretended to fire a barrage of arrows out over the fields. He put his hand flat over his eyes as if watching the arrow's progress. Then – "Oh no!" he cried, and he clutched at his chest, gasped and fell backwards, as if the arrows had turned round in the air and returned to hit him!

Bad Boyz' next stop was in Menuer itself, where they'd been invited to an official reception at the town hall, hosted by the mayor. Their opponents were there too and there was much nodding and hand-shaking. The mayor made a short welcoming speech in broken English. He said he was sorry that Bad Boyz were having such bad times in France, but he supposed that they were used to it, because they always had bad times in England. Bad Boyz were rather confused by this remark – until Mr Davies explained that the mayor had actually been talking about the weather. In French, he said, the word *temps* meant both times and weather and the mayor had chosen the wrong one.

After a muted beginning, the reception went well, and when Bad Boyz returned to the farm that night, their spirits had lifted considerably. Bloomer wanted to go and see Vincent's rabbit, while Dareth and Max were keen to go for a splash about in the boat.

"In the morning," said Mr Davies. "I want you all in bed now. We've got another big game tomorrow."

The only one whose mood had shown no improvement since the afternoon was Sadiq. He'd barely spoken since the match and by bedtime looked more glum than ever. Miss Rogers suggested that the two of them went for a walk round the farmyard while the others got ready for bed. Sadiq didn't exactly turn somersaults of delight, but he did follow her. Mr Davies crossed his fingers...

About half an hour later, the walkers returned and Miss Rogers settled Sadiq in bed before returning to the farmhouse.

"Well?" Mr Davies asked expectantly.

"He's very homesick, poor boy," said Miss Rogers. "He had a good cry and that seemed to make him feel better. I could see he was upset, but he didn't want to break down in front of the others." She shook her head. "You boys," she laughed.

"We're very sensitive," said Mr Davies. Then he considered this statement for a moment, thinking about Dareth, Kyle, Max... "Well, some of us are," he added.

10 ⚽

Dear Nan

Here I am in France. The picher is
of a famus battlefild where the English
gave the French a good beeting. It was
the archers that done it. And I don't
mean that radio program that you like!
Yesterday we playd a mach and got
beet 4-0. Boo. Hiss. This morning we
had an egg fight. It was wicked. I had
egg all in me hair and me ears and
everyfing. Wish you was here (but I
bet you don't!). See you soon

Dareth

Ps love to Rameses!

No one was quite sure who started the egg fight – or at least no one admitted to it. The farmer's children had been sent out to collect the eggs for breakfast and they'd invited their guests to join them. One thing led to another, and when Mr Davies emerged from the farmhouse a little while later, it was, for the second day running, to the sounds of wild screeching and shouting. The rumpus wasn't in the water this time, though, but by the henhouse. No sooner had the Bad Boyz coach set off to investigate when Max appeared, followed closely by a flying egg. An instant later the egg cracked against the back of Max's head. He threw himself to the ground, howling with laughing, while a glob of yolk ran down his neck. Mr Davies started to run…

The scene that met him was one of complete and utter mess. All of the children – French and English – were gathered in a small area in front of the henhouse. They were in a state of giggling hysteria and all splattered with egg. Dareth, Kyle and Louis appeared to have got the worst of it. They were eggy from head to toe. The ground around them was littered with broken eggshell and shiny with egg white and yolk.

Madame Champs was not amused. "Your breakfast is finished," she said. "We 'ave no more eggs."

The children were sent off to clean themselves up and change their clothes. Then they were assembled in the large farmhouse kitchen, where Monsieur Champs gave them all a stern lecture on irresponsible behaviour – supported by Mr Davies, who made each of his players apologize personally to Monsieur and Madame Champs for their part in the egg fight. Then all the children were made to clear up the mess they had made.

Bad Boyz were genuinely sorry for upsetting Monsieur and Madame Champs, but they couldn't feel sorry for the fight itself: it had just been too much fun. Even as they were clearing up, they couldn't help joking about it.

"Do you know," Max said, "that was the most *eggs*iting fight I've ever had."

"*Eggs*actly," agreed Dareth.

"It was *eggs*traordinary," Jordan added.

And so it went on.

The egg fight had one very positive result,

though: it cheered Sadiq up and made him forget about his homesickness – and his unfortunate own goal the day before. He spent most of the morning with a broad smile on his face. Sung-Woo helped here too; of all the Bad Boyz he seemed the most sensitive to what Sadiq was experiencing. When the clearing up was done, he offered Sadiq his Gameboy and the two of them spent a happy couple of hours together playing on it.

So, after its frenetic beginning, the morning passed peacefully enough. But there was more drama to come.

When Vincent went to feed his rabbit just before lunch, he discovered an empty cage. Caramel had gone! A frantic search followed.

They'd been hunting round the farm for a while when Jordan suddenly had a thought.

"Where's Bloomer?" she said.

No one knew. In fact, he hadn't been seen since they'd finished clearing up the mess a couple of hours earlier.

"He said he was going to lie down for a bit," Kyle recalled.

Jordan went to look for him.

Sure enough, there he was, tucked up in bed.

"Are you all right, Bloomer?" Jordan asked.

"Yeah," Bloomer piped. He stretched and yawned. "I'm just having a little rest."

Jordan told him about Vincent's rabbit going missing. "You haven't seen it, have you?" she asked.

Bloomer's cheeks flushed pink. "Me?" he said. "Why me?"

"Because you're the one who likes it so much," Jordan pointed out.

"Yeah, well," Bloomer squeaked. "That doesn't mean I've seen it, does it?"

Something wriggled under the blanket on Bloomer's bed. Then it wriggled again. Bloomer stared at the blanket. Jordan stared at Bloomer.

"Bloomer, there wouldn't be a rabbit in your bed by any chance, would there?" she enquired casually.

Bloomer's blush grew deeper. "I just wanted to play with it for a bit. I was going to put it back," he insisted.

Minutes later, Caramel was back in the arms of his fretful owner.

For the second time that morning Bloomer got a telling off. "You can't just take other

58

people's property like that without asking, Bloomer," Mr Davies told him. Bloomer looked suitably sorry. Fortunately, Vincent was very understanding. He was delighted to have his rabbit back and seemed quite pleased that it was Bloomer, a fellow rabbit-lover, who had taken it. He invited Bloomer to go with him back to the rabbit cage and feed Caramel.

"They're very sweet, aren't they?" Miss Rogers remarked as the two small boys walked off together.

Mr Davies laughed. "Careful what you say," he said. "You'll ruin my team's reputation."

11

After a hearty and much-appreciated lunch, Bad Boyz and their hosts set off for the second match between the two little league champions.

It was a relief to everyone that the sky was blue and the clouds white and high. It wasn't exactly hot, but it was pleasantly warm.

If anything, the crowd at this second match was even bigger than at the first – no doubt due to the change in the weather and the home team's fine win the day before. But Bad Boyz were prepared this time. The big crowd didn't phase them as it had the previous day. Even in their warming up they looked a lot more purposeful.

The pitch was soft but not slippery – the only sign of the heavy rain that had fallen just twenty-four hours ago was a single puddle halfway between one of the penalty areas and the centre circle. Max managed to land in it, though, even before the match had kicked off.

As usual with Max, however, once the game did kick off the clowning stopped and he was fiercely competitive. He broke up two attacks in the first five minutes with perfectly timed but bone-jarring tackles. On the other side of the defence, Sadiq was equally uncompromising. He sent Louis sprawling with a hard but fair challenge. The crowd oohed, but the referee waved play on and Sadiq helped Louis up with a smile.

The spirit between the two teams was very good, but this match was much tougher than the first. This was a game that they both really wanted to win.

It was Les Bleus who got the first break – and a lucky break it was. A long-range shot from Louis deflected off Jordan and fell straight in front of Laura just a few metres from goal. Kyle threw himself to make a save, but he couldn't keep the girl's shot out. Bad Boyz were a goal down.

The pleasing thing for Mr Davies was the way his team responded. Their heads didn't go down. Quite the opposite, in fact. They attacked the French team with even more urgency. As the half progressed, Bad Boyz were well on top. Dareth hit the post, Sung-Woo shot just wide, the French keeper nearly punched the ball into his own goal... Finally, with one minute of the first half remaining, Jordan struck the equalizer, after an exchange of passes with Dareth. It was no less than Bad Boyz deserved.

Mr Davies's half-time talk was full of praise and encouragement. If they kept that up he'd be happy, he said.

Miss Rogers had a few quiet words with Sadiq, just to check he was OK.

"I'm fine," he said with unusual cheeriness. "I'm not sure about Louis, though."

Bad Boyz were eager to get started again, but they had to wait a bit longer than expected. This was because a duck had waddled onto the pitch at half-time and sat down in the puddle. When the teams came back for the second half, the duck stayed where it was and showed no signs of wanting to move. It took several attempts to shoo it away.

"I've heard of dog on the pitch stopping play," Mr Davies said. "But duck on the pitch is a new one on me."

"Yeah," Max agreed. He threw his hands in the air. "It's quackers!"

At last the second half got underway, and it was every bit as hard-fought as the first. The two girls on the pitch were playing particularly well. Having both scored, they were full of confidence and at the heart of their teams' best moves. Laura's precise through-ball very nearly set up Louis for a clear run on goal; only a last-ditch interception by Sadiq averted the danger. At the other end, Jordan's clever reverse pass should have given Bloomer a great chance to score, if a plane hadn't flown over at that moment and caused him to lose concentration.

As in the first half, though, Bad Boyz gradually gained the upper hand. They started to pin the home team back in their own half. The pressure mounted and mounted. The crowd's shouting became more desperate. Every clearance was greeted with a cheer of relief. But then the ball came back again...

At last the pressure told. Dareth sold his marker a dummy with a sweetly executed step-over, then slid the ball through a narrow gap between two defenders, to Sung-Woo. The striker's first touch was perfect, knocking the ball nicely ahead of him, but well short of the keeper. A sprint, a shuffle to the right and a crisp side-footed shot and the ball was in the net. For the first time in either match, Bad Boyz were in the lead – and it was a lead they were determined to hold onto.

The home team rallied bravely and tried to push forward, but their efforts were weary and lacked bite. In the end, it was Bad Boyz who scored to wrap up a fine victory and the scorer, to everyone's delight, was Sadiq. He thumped a rocket of a shot high into the net after Dareth's corner had been nodded across the goal by Jordan. It was rare indeed for Sadiq to score and he celebrated like it was his birthday, Christmas and the end of term all in one!

"I don't think we'll need to worry about Sadiq tonight," Miss Rogers murmured to Mr Davies.

"No," the coach nodded.

Moments later, the final whistle blew. Bad Boyz had beaten Les Bleus 3–1 and the series was drawn, one win each. Honours were even. The players and managers of both sides shook hands, while the crowd applauded. Football and friendship were the winners, everyone agreed.

Watching his team's extravagant, joyful, slightly daft celebrations (at that instant they were miming firing arrows into the air), Mr Davies was filled with a sudden feeling of deep satisfaction. Kyle, Dareth, Bloomer, Jordan, Sadiq, Max, Sung-Woo... Home or away, Bad Boyz were wild, they were trouble, but they were a great bunch and he was hugely proud of his barmy army and what they'd achieved.

The football was over. Now, *mes choux*, it was time to party...

Follow Bad Boyz on their
Little League Cup run in:

K.O. KINGS

(Turn the page to read the first chapter.)

"Catch it, Kyle, you big blob!"

The Bad Boyz keeper turned and glared at the shouting figure on the touch-line. He'd just palmed a fierce shot round the post and he reckoned it had been a pretty good save.

"Don't take any notice," said Jordan. She clapped a hand on Kyle's broad shoulder. "That was wicked."

"Who *is* that geezer, anyway?" growled Sadiq, waving a clenched fist towards the touch-line.

"Yeah, who's he calling a big blob?" said Max. "Great ugly gorilla." He put his hands in his armpits, pulled a face and started making gorilla noises. Next to him, Bloomer squeaked with laughter and joined in. They were still monkeying around when the corner came over. Luckily, Dareth, the captain, was paying attention to the game and booted the ball clear.

"Come on, Bad Boyz! Concentrate!" called Mr Davies. He was both the Bad Boyz manager and a teacher at their school. He glanced along the touch-line. He was used to being his team's only supporter and he wondered who the man was who'd shouted at Kyle.

Mr Davies had never seen him before, but he was obviously someone who knew Kyle well. All his comments had been directed at the keeper – and none had been complimentary. Fortunately, Kyle was in a pretty good mood. The match was almost over and he hadn't let in a goal. At the other end, Bad Boyz had struck three times and were well set for a comfortable win.

It was the first round of the Appleton Little League Cup. Bad Boyz' opponents were X Club 7. In his pre-match team talk, Mr Davies had called them "the most improved team in the league".

"Yeah," Dareth had agreed. "But they're still pants."

They'd looked anything but pants in the first half, though. The game had been very even and Kyle had had to make a number of fine saves – though none of them good enough for the man on the touch-line, it seemed. When Kyle parried the ball, he should have caught it; when he saved with his feet, he should have used his hands; when he booted the ball clear, he should have picked it up...

By half-time, only one goal had separated the teams – and that had been a fluke. A corner from Jordan had rebounded off the post, hit a defender on the heel and bounced back over the line.

In the second half, though, Bad Boyz had been well on top. Sung-Woo, their main striker, had scored twice and could have got three or four more. Jordan had hit the post with a scorching shot and Dareth had had a header cleared off the line.

To their credit, X Club 7 carried on battling to the end, even though they were obviously very tired. It was due to this tiredness that they gave away a penalty in the last minute. A weary defender stumbled and tripped Sung-Woo as the striker chased a long kick from

Kyle. It was a clear penalty.

Dareth offered the ball to Sung-Woo. "You take it," he said. "Get your hat-trick."

But Sung-Woo shook his head with a characteristic frown. "You the penalty taker," he insisted. "I have two goals already. You score."

Dareth shrugged. "All right. Cheers!" he said.

He placed the ball on the spot and took a couple of steps backwards. Then he trotted forward and blasted it into the top right-hand corner of the net. At once he wheeled round and began his latest celebration. This involved cupping one hand round his ear and flapping the other like a wing. He was well into this before he noticed that no one else was joining in. They were all just standing looking at him.

Dareth's hands dropped and so did his smile. "Wassup?" he said, puzzled.

Jordan nodded towards the goal. "Look," she said.

Dareth turned. The referee was still standing by the penalty spot with his arms folded. "Take it again," he ordered. "And this time, wait till I blow my whistle."

"I thought you did blow," said Dareth.

The referee shook his head.

Dareth grinned. "Must have been Bloomer, then," he said.

Once more he placed the ball on the penalty spot.

Once more he took a couple of steps back.

He waited.

The referee blew his whistle.

Once more, Dareth ran forward and blasted the ball … but this time into the top left-hand corner.

He raised his hands and started to turn, but before he could, Bloomer and Max had jumped him. A moment later, Kyle tumbled on top and all four fell in a screeching heap.

The mystery man on the touch-line was not amused. "Get back in goal, Kyle, you idiot!" he barked. "The game's not over!" But he was wrong. For at that instant the referee blew the final whistle.

Bad Boyz had beaten X Club 7 by 4–0 – the same score as in the league. They were through to the next round of the cup.

Author's Note

Although Appleton Little League is my own creation, it's based on an organization that really exists. Little League Football is a registered charity that provides free football for children from eight to thirteen years old in over thirty leagues around the country. The emphasis is on enthusiasm and effort rather than ability – players are encouraged to develop team spirit, self-discipline and sportsmanship. It's also a lot of fun and a good place to start playing organized football. Players join individually rather than as a team, as in my series, but most of the rules are as I've described them. If you want to find out more, check out the Little League Football website:
www.littleleaguefootball.com

There may be a league on your doorstep!

If you're interested in joining a Sunday junior football team, a useful site to look at is:
www.juniorleague.net

It has details of teams and leagues right across the country.

If you like playing football, there's a team out there for you!

To ask Alan Durant anything about the Bad Boyz series – or any football matter – you can contact him by e-mail at:
alan.durant@walker.co.uk

He'd love to hear from you!